playground

MALAIKA RO⟨S⟩

MAN HUNT

ORCHARD BOOKS

Orchard Books
96 Leonard Street, London EC2A 4RH
Orchard Books Australia
14 Mars Road, Lane Cove, NSW 2066
1 86039 215 6 (hardback)
1 86039 232 6 (paperback)
First published in Great Britain 1996
First paperback publication 1996

A CIP catalogue record for this book is available from the
British Library.

Printed in Great Britain

For Garikai and Danjuma
and for the friends who showed me the way.

Chapter One

MAX GLARED AT the TV screen. Then he glared at his big, bossy sister sitting at the other end of the faded sofa.

"D'you know what we need?" said Max. "A man! What we need is a man."

"Shush," said Claire. "I'm trying to watch the film."

"If we had a man," said Max, "we'd be watching 'Match of the Day' on the other side. It's a 'Road to Wembley' special – fourth round of the FA cup."

"Shush!" said Claire.

"At this rate," said Max, "I'll be the last *Young Gunner* in the whole of the universe to find out the result."

He glared at the television again. The adverts were coming on. The screen filled up with doctors, truckers, pilots, miners and firefighters. All brave, handsome and clean-shaven.

"Looks more like an advert for men than razor blades," said Max. "If you just want to ogle men we could turn over. There are twenty-two of them on the other side playing soccer."

Claire whirled round and her pony-tail flew up into the air. She peered out at him from behind her fringe.

"Just . . . shut . . . up," she hissed.

No problem, thought Max. Good idea. All this talk's getting us nowhere.

He watched her out of the corner of his eye and imagined the chops and changes he'd make, if he ever got the chance. For a start, he'd chop off that pony-tail. Then he'd change that silly frock for a decent pair of jeans or tracksuit bottoms. Maybe he'd just trade her in for a brother!

The film came back on and Max waited for Claire to relax and loosen her grip on the remote control. When the moment came, he leapt across the sofa and snatched it away. He jabbed at the buttons and punched the air in triumph, as he saw a quick flash of red and white and heard the roar of the crowd.

But the red and white blurred into pink, as Claire lunged back at him. She wrestled him to the floor and sat on top of him.

"Get off!" he cried. "You're hurting me."

To his surprise, she rolled off him on to the threadbare carpet. Then he saw why. Mum was standing in the doorway, wrapped in a bath towel. Her face was bright red and she was frowning.

Claire groaned and Max turned to look at her. She was rolling around the floor as if she was in agony.

It was an old trick. He'd seen it loads of times before. He'd even fallen for it a couple of times. But Mum never seemed to learn. She took one look at Claire and started yelling at Max.

"How many times do I have to tell you? No fighting with your sister! What was it this time? Television, I bet. Well, I've had enough, Max. Go to your room!"

Max opened his mouth ready to argue.

"No arguments!" said Mum, as she hitched up her towel and helped Claire up on to the sofa.

"It's not fair!" shouted Max. "You're always on her side. You always stick up for her."

"Oh, Max," said Mum. "Don't be so . . ."

"It's true," said Max. "And I know why too. It's because she's a girl. You girls always stick together."

Mum smiled. She put her hand over her mouth to try and hide it but she was too slow. Max had already seen.

He felt a rush of anger. Then he stormed out of the living room and slammed the door.

Alone in his bedroom, Max tried not to think about how lonely he felt. It wasn't just about being the only boy. Sometimes, he realised, it was about being a *black* boy – with a white mother and a white sister!

Claire's dad was white and Mum had left him before Claire was even born. His own father was black but Mum hadn't bothered to marry him either and in the end, she left him too.

It was late when he heard Mum creep into his room. He pretended to be asleep.

"G'night, Max," she whispered.

She kissed him on the cheek, then tiptoed away, leaving the smell of soap behind.

She must be joking, thought Max. I'm not making friends yet. Besides, I've got some serious thinking to do. I have to make plans for a man hunt.

Chapter Two

"You have to get up," said Claire.

"What for?" said Max. "It's Sunday."

He pulled the covers up over his head.

All night long, he'd been dreaming about adverts for men. Not just on the telly. They'd been everywhere – newspapers, posters, hot-air balloons, flashing neon lights in Piccadilly Circus!

'BARGAINS GALORE – CUT-PRICE MEN!'

Just minutes before, he'd been rushing around Tesco's trying to buy one! He was exhausted.

"The Cavendishes are coming up for breakfast," said Claire.

Max shot out from under the quilt, suddenly wide awake.

"Oh, no! You're kidding!"

" 'Fraid not," said Claire, with a grin.

Max buried his head in the pillow. The *Dishes*

would bring the female head-count to five. He didn't think he could take it.

"What time are they coming?"

"Not sure. Eleven, I think."

Max looked at the Arsenal clock on the chair next to his bed. Ten forty-two. He leapt out of bed, threw on his clothes and ran down to the kitchen.

Mum was bright red again. She was taking bread rolls out of the oven.

"Hi," she said brightly. "How're you doing?"

Her glasses steamed up and she wiped them on her T-shirt. It was green and baggy with words on the front. Max already knew what they said, but he read them anyway:

'A woman without a man is like a fish without a bicycle'.

"I'm fine," he sighed. "Listen, Mum. Can I go round to Denzil's? I need him to help me with . . . with something."

"I don't suppose this has got anything to do with Shirl and the girls coming for breakfast, has it?" said Mum. "Shirley-Anne's my friend, y'know, not just a neighbour. You could try and make a bit of an effort."

She paused and handed him some hot rolls.

"You'd better get going," she warned, "before I change my mind."

Max met the Cavendishes on his way out of the flats. He decided to make an effort. He flashed them a smile.

"Mornin', Shirley-Anne. Hello, Charlotte. Hello, Sugar."

They were obviously impressed. Charlotte and Sugar gaped, open-mouthed. Mrs Cavendish wobbled on her high heels and tripped over.

"For heaven's sake, Max," she squealed. "Look what you've done. I've broken a nail!"

"Mum'll fix it," said Max. "She's got some of those plastic ones from work."

He dazzled them with another smile and raced down the steps into the street.

He didn't stop running until he reached Denzil's house. By the time he staggered into the room which Denzil shared with his baby brothers, he felt as if his lungs had burst.

"Oh, boy," he gasped, when he could finally speak. "I'm glad you're back."

"Me too," said Denzil, his brown face splitting

into a wide grin. "I've been chucked round Birmingham like pass-the-parcel. First Uncle Courtney, then my grandma's and then Uncle Claude's. Uncle Errol was s'posed to bring me back but his car broke down so Dad had to drive the van up to fetch me."

He dropped to the floor and picked up his computer joystick.

"Uncles," said Max, thoughtfully.

"What?" said Denzil.

"Uncles," said Max. "D'you think any of your uncles would marry my mum?"

"What're you on about?" said Denzil.

"Men!" said Max. "Boys and men! You've got loads in your family and *I* haven't got any. I'm the only one!"

Denzil put down the joystick and turned off the computer.

"You missed the match again, didn't you?"

"Goal!" said Max. "Got it in one. But that's not why I'm here. I'm going on a man hunt – and I need you to help me."

"Your mum'll never get married," said Denzil. "She's a feminist."

"Are you going to help me or not?" said Max.

" 'Course I am," said Denzil. "I'll get some paper. We can make a list of possibles and put them in order, like the league tables. All we have to do then is get your mum off with whoever comes out top."

Chapter Three

AT SCHOOL THE next day, Denzil was again writing busily. So were most of the others in the class. A few, like Max, sucked the ends of their pens and gazed into space.

Max gazed at the zig-zag pattern shaved on to the back of Denzil's head. Uncle Errol was a brilliant barber, but in the husband-for-mum league tables, he'd come second from bottom!

Max scratched the back of his own head and felt the wild mop of dark brown curls.

It's a shame, he thought. I could've had a decent haircut for once, instead of being dragged off to Mum's salon.

The other uncles had done OK, but somehow *Mr Goddard* had come out on top. Max closed his eyes and ran an action replay.

"He's too old," Max had said.

"Just grown-up," said Denzil.

"More like stuck-up," said Max.

"He's just a bit posh," said Denzil.

"And he's got bad breath," said Max.

"He just needs a new toothbrush," said Denzil.

"But he's the Deputy Head!" Max had shouted.

"Good job. Loads of money," said Denzil. "You have to look at it from your mum's point of view."

Max had given up, but he was having second thoughts about it now. He was desperate to get a man into his life. But was he desperate enough for Mr Goddard?

"Max . . . Max Thompson!"

He looked up.

"Yes, Miss."

"How much have you written?"

Max looked at the blank page in front of him.

"I'm still thinking, Miss."

"Thinking?" said Miss Finch, as if she didn't know what it was. "Well, bless my soul. Think fast, Max. Think fast."

Max scribbled his name at the top of the paper. He copied the date and the title from the blackboard. Monday 21 February. My Half-term Holiday.

Then he threw down his pen in disgust. How could anyone write *two* full pages about a *one*-week holiday?

He folded his arms and leaned back until his chair was balancing on two legs. Mohin and Paul Kelly, he noticed, were both staring at him. They were probably thinking he'd lost his mind.

He hadn't. His mind was busy and he was thinking fast, just like Miss Finch had said.

Parents' evening was months away and Max had been wondering how on earth he was going to get Mum and Mr Goddard together. Now, suddenly, he knew what to do – nothing! Absolutely nothing.

Miss Finch kept him in at break-time but afterwards when she came to collect his work, his paper was still almost empty.

"Max," she said gently. "What's going on?"

"Nothing, Miss," said Max.

Miss Finch stopped smiling. Her papery grey cheeks turned pink. Her hands fluttered. She looked like a baby bird frightened of learning to fly.

"Dearie me," she said. "It's not the sort of nothing I want in my classroom, Max. You pull your socks up or I'll have to send you to Mr Goddard."

This is working like a dream, thought Max. What a goal!

But Miss Finch was patient. She didn't yell at him, like Mum. She put up with his blank pieces of paper and his one-word answers right up until home-time.

By then, her cheeks were bright red and her arms were almost flapping. She was finally ready for take-off and at last things got moving.

Mr Goddard gave Max a note to take home to Mum and while he bawled at him in the office, Max got the chance to take a closer look at him.

He was round and fat and each time he spoke, his enormous belly and his double chins wobbled in perfect time with the words.

"I won't stand for it!" *Wobble, wobble.*

"D'you understand?" *Wobble, wobble.*

To be fair, Mr Goddard knew his stuff when it came to football. But he didn't seem a bit like the sort of man Mum would want to marry! Max was having serious doubts, but it was too late to back out. All he could do now was wait.

Chapter Four

MAX WAITED FOR two whole days.

On Wednesday evening, he was in his room trying to learn how to spell *inauspicious* when he heard Mum come crashing into the flat like a ballistic missile.

"Max!" she bellowed. "Get down here!"

Max dragged himself down the stairs as slowly as he could, but he still reached the living room in about ten seconds flat. He stood close to the door, in case he needed to make a quick getaway.

Mum was pouring herself a drink and boy, did she look mad! He shuddered as he watched her gulp down a huge mouthful of wine.

"Who does that awful man think he is?" she yelled. "His name's Goddard not God!"

Max stared. There were drops of blood down the front of her blouse! He had a terrible vision of Mum and Mr Goddard in a punch-up. She must have clocked him one and made his nose bleed.

"Pompous old fuddy-duddy!" Mum was saying. "Telling me how to bring up my kids. Bad manners, I call it – and bad breath!"

She spluttered as she took another big swig of red wine, and wiped a trickle from her chin.

"Why don't you sit down, Mum?" said Max. "You look tired. I can do the dinner."

It didn't take him long. They were having left-overs. In the kitchen, Max pushed the defrost and re-heat buttons on the microwave – and pulled himself together.

OK, the wedding was off – but Mr Goddard was to blame for that. He should have known better than to be rude to Mum. Even so, Max was shocked. Bad manners and fighting were not what he expected from parents and teachers.

"I saw Miss Finch as well as Mr Goddard," said Mum, when they'd eaten. "Poor old dear. Shaking like a leaf, she was. Her nerves must be shot to pieces."

Here it comes, thought Max, feeling a bit guilty. It's me against a poor old biddy now, not a pompous old fuddy-duddy. I'll be grounded for the rest of my life.

"You're grounded," said Mum. "For the rest of the week!"

"Better than a life sentence," muttered Max, "or a public hanging at dawn."

"I'm not joking, Max," said Mum. "There's to be no football either, until Miss Finch tells me you're back to normal."

Max felt himself go cold.

"But Mum," he pleaded. "I've got a match tomorrow and I'm going to Highbury with Denzil's dad to see Arsenal on Saturday."

"No arguments!" said Mum. "I'm too tired. I'm going to have a bath."

Max kicked the back of the sofa and Mum poked her head back round the door just in time to see him doing it.

"I'm working an extra shift at the salon this Saturday," she said, through gritted teeth, "and Claire's going ice-skating. You'll have to stay with Shirl and the girls now you're not going to see the football."

Max kicked the sofa again and this time Claire poked her big nose round the door.

"You never know," she smirked. "She might forget all about it before Saturday. I'm making her a cup of tea. D'you want one?"

Max wasn't sure if she was trying to cheer him up, but tea was the last thing he needed. What he needed right now was a miracle!

"Don't bother!" he fumed, and stomped up to his room to finish learning his spellings.

There was no miracle, of course, and Mum did not forget. She had a memory like an IBM computer. And Max reckoned she must have phoned round half the universe to make sure no one else would forget either.

Mr Goddard gave Max's place on the soccer team to Sugar of all people, and Mr Moses – Denzil's dad – said he hoped Max wasn't going to turn out to be a bad influence.

What a cheek! None of this would have happened without Denzil's dopey ideas. And to make things even worse, Denzil got to see a brilliant home win for Arsenal, while he was stuck at home with Madam Cavendish!

Still, Max realised, when the week was finally over, it wasn't all bad. For a start, he came top in the spelling test, which wasn't exactly *normal* but it was enough to get Mum and Miss Finch off his back.

Second – and this was the best bit – he came up with a brilliant phase-two plan for the man hunt.

Chapter Five

"ADVERTISE!" SAID MAX. "I think we should advertise."

Denzil shifted his bag to the other shoulder and kept on walking. It was Monday again, and they were on the way home from school.

"Well," said Max. "What d'you think?"

"Where are you going to put an advert for a man?" said Denzil. "On the telly?"

"Too expensive," said Max.

"Where then?" said Denzil.

"Follow me," said Max. "I'll show you."

He led the way to Hornby's General Stores and stopped in front of the window.

"Look at those postcards," he said, pointing. "They're all adverts."

Denzil was silent as he stared through the glass and read some of them.

"You're off your trolley!" he said, after a few minutes. "You can't advertise here. It's full of ads for lost dogs and kittens for sale and rooms to rent."

"And *wanted* ads," said Max.

"Right," grinned Denzil. "Look at this one. Wanted – chair for lady with wooden legs and leather bottom!"

Max couldn't see the joke. But right there on the pavement, in full view of everyone, Denzil doubled up and howled. He sounded just like Sugar that time Max had fallen off his bike and she laughed so much she wet herself!

Max walked away, hoping the same thing would happen to Denzil.

"Max! Max, wait for me," yelled Denzil.

Max walked faster.

"I wasn't laughing at you," said Denzil, when he caught up. "It's just . . . well, you know – lost dogs and all that."

"It's not that far off, when you think about it, is it?" said Max. "Lost dogs, lost dads – what's the difference?"

"Come on," said Denzil, and at last he stopped

grinning. "Why don't you come back to my place? I've just thought of something."

Max heard himself say "OK" – and made a mental note to get his head tested.

When they arrived, Denzil's mum was trying to squeeze the twins into their high chairs.

"Max! Denny!" she beamed. "You're just in time for dinner."

It was what she always said. You could drop in here at midnight, thought Max, and you'd still be in time for dinner.

Afterwards, when he was stuffed to the neck with saltfish and dumplings, Denzil presented him with an old newspaper, as if it was a first edition Superman comic.

"The *Parkway Gazette*!" said Max. "What use is this?"

Denzil flicked over the pages until he found the one headed 'Lonely Hearts'.

"My mum's not lonely," said Max. "She practically *lives* with Sugar Dish's mum and she's got loads of other friends."

"I know," said Denzil, "but this is full of women

who are looking for men – and men who are looking for women."

Max wasn't convinced, but he scanned the columns of tiny print.

He tried to picture Mum with a quiet, lonely widower interested in classical music. No chance! Mum was loud. She liked Meatloaf and Tina Turner. She'd eat him for breakfast!

He tried another one: 'Handsome young prince seeks plump princess, no children.' Fat chance! Mum was as skinny as a bean-pole and what was she supposed to do with him and Claire? He quickly read a few more but none of them looked promising.

Then he had an idea.

"I'll put my own advert in," he said.

Denzil was grinning again. "It costs ten pounds for twenty words."

"Ten pounds!" said Max. "Where am I s'posed to find ten pounds?"

"I spent all my money in Birmingham," said Denzil, "but I've got 26p you can have."

"Denzil Moses – soccer superstar, genius and millionaire," said Max, laughing at last.

Later, at home, Max emptied out the contents of

his cash box. Then he scratched around in the dust and biscuit crumbs down the back of the sofa. The grand total came to £5.37.

Miles off! For a while, he thought about asking Mum or Claire for a loan. Then he thought a bit more and decided not to. They were sure to start asking all sorts of awkward questions. He couldn't risk it. He had to find a way to deal with the advert on his own.

Chapter Six

THE *PARKWAY GAZETTE* offices were hidden in an alley behind the High Street.

The next evening, Max walked past the shabby front door three times before he plucked up the courage to open it and go inside. When he did, the noise from the printing presses threatened to deafen him.

"Oy!" shouted a voice in his ear. "D'you want something?"

Max turned and looked into the face of an old man who wasn't much taller than himself. Three warts, a piggy nose and a ginger moustache. It was the only hair he had. His shiny bald head was half hidden by a woolly hat and lower down, he was wearing filthy overalls and green wellies.

"Yes," yelled Max above the din. "I want to put an advert in the paper."

The man said something which Max couldn't hear, but at the last moment he jerked his head towards some stairs.

Max raced up, two at a time, then stopped. There was a whole row of closed doors but the only one with a sign said 'fire exit'.

He was about to turn the handle on the first door when it flew open and almost yanked off his arm.

"Clear off, you little creep!" said the woman responsible. "This is the ladies' loo. The gents' is down the hall."

"I don't need to go!" shouted Max. "I want to put an advert in the paper."

It was much quieter up here, but he'd forgotten to adjust his volume control. The woman stuffed her fingers in her ears. Judging by the length of her nails, Max reckoned she was in danger of puncturing both ear drums.

"I'm not deaf," she said.

Not yet, Max thought. But you soon will be if you carry on doing that.

"Last door on the left," said the woman, pulling out a bright pink claw and pointing.

Max felt like making a run for it and getting out

of there while he still had the chance but he forced himself to walk along the corridor and open the door.

"Hello there, laddie. Can I help you?"

Max sighed with relief. It wasn't a dungeon or a torture chamber after all. It was a normal office with filing cabinets and spider plants in plastic pots. And a normal man in a business suit, sitting behind a desk.

"Angus McDonald – Advertising, Sales and Distribution Manager," said the man.

He stood up and shook Max's hand. He was tall with dark brown wavy hair, light brown skin and smily eyes.

"Can I help you, laddie?" he said again.

I hope so, thought Max, after all the trouble I've gone to.

"I want to put an advert in the paper," he said.

"Classified or display?" said Angus.

"Er . . . Lonely Hearts," said Max.

"You're a wee bit young to be wanting a lassie," said Angus, with a smile.

"Mmm, I know," said Max, "but I have to find a man for my mother and . . well, I was wondering if we could make a deal."

"Let me guess," said Angus. "You want to even

the score. I bet you've a whole crowd of sisters who're giving you a hard time."

"Only one," said Max, surprised.

"Aye. It was the same for me when I was a lad," said Angus. "What's the deal then?"

"A half-price deal," said Max, looking down at his trainers. "I've got enough for ten words with 37p left over, but I could throw that in on top to make it worth your while."

He glanced up at Angus just as his smile faded and was replaced by a deep frown. His whole face seemed to droop.

After a few seconds, Max felt his own face crumple with disappointment, and he turned to leave.

"Got it!" said Angus suddenly. "D'you know how to use a computer?"

Max nodded.

But I need a man, he thought, not a job!

"A do-it-yourself deal," smiled Angus. "Get your advert tapped in over there and I'll let you have it for half-price. If you get cracking, we'll get it in this week's paper. It comes out the day after tomorrow."

Max smiled to himself. He'd scored another goal! Bargains galore – cut-price men!

Chapter Seven

'THE DAY AFTER tomorrow' was Thursday.

"We'll have to sneak out," said Denzil at lunch-time.

"Sneak out!" yelled Max, glancing up at the iron railings and imagining barbed wire.

"Shut up!" said Denzil. "They'll hear you."

Max turned around. Armed guards disguised as dinner ladies were patrolling the playground. They probably had grenades tucked inside their knickers.

He lowered his voice. "You're crazy. We can't sneak out. We'd never make it."

"Come on," urged Denzil. "We're only nipping down to the shops. We haven't got any money left so we can't *buy* the paper. If we wait till home-time, the shop'll be packed and you'll never get a look at it."

"And I'll miss soccer practice again," admitted

Max. "But how do we do it? We'll have to tunnel our way out."

"There's a hole in the fence behind the toilets," said Denzil. "All you have to do is take a deep breath, hold your nose and squeeze through. There's no tunnelling involved."

Max fiddled with the zip on his *Gunners* jacket while he thought it over.

"OK," he said doubtfully, "but we'd better not get caught. If my mum ever finds out about this, she'll kill me!"

"Don't worry," said Denzil, as they headed off towards the toilets. "Trust me. When we get to the shop, I'll go in first and create a diversion. Then you nip in behind me and have a look at the advert. Old Hornblower won't even notice you're there."

Max almost changed his mind and turned back at the thought of Mr Hornby. He was a real misery-guts with bulging dead-fish eyes and thin grey lips that never smiled.

"The Hornblower notices everything," said Max gloomily as they reached the shop.

Denzil ignored him. He was already pushing open the door. Then – in exactly the same way that he took a penalty kick – he skipped into the shop and took an almighty right-foot swing against the base of a revolving card stand.

Max dived head-first through the door after him and scrambled behind the rack of high shelves that ran down the middle of the shop. He held his breath and waited for the card stand to clatter to the ground.

It didn't. Somehow, the Hornblower must have pulled off a brilliant save. Only now he was bellowing at Denzil as if the whole shop had been demolished.

"You stupid idiot!" he roared. "Can't you be more careful?"

Max suddenly remembered to breathe again. He sucked in a huge mouthful of air and looked around anxiously. He was right beside the low shelf that held the newspapers and unless Mr Hornby's fish-eyes could see *through* tinned prunes and pickled onions, he was safe. Well, safer than Denzil anyway.

Quickly, he stretched out his hand, pulled down a *Parkway Gazette* and began searching for the 'Lonely Hearts'.

Just as he found the right page, another loud voice on the other side of the prunes made him freeze and left him gasping for breath again.

"For heaven's sake," screeched the voice. "It was an accident. Leave the boy alone."

No, thought Max. No! It can't be . . .

Slowly, carefully, he stood up and peered between the cartons and cans on the top shelf.

It was! It was Shirley-Anne Cavendish and she was jabbing her plastic fingernail into Mr Hornby's chest and giving him the telling off of his life!

Two other customers were gaping at Shirley-Anne with their mouths open. Denzil was nowhere to be seen.

"The customer," shrieked Shirley-Anne, "is *always* right!"

Max felt a terrible stab of panic as he sank back on to the floor. Even if Mr Hornby missed him, Shirley-Anne was sure to spot him. She'd tell Mum. His life would be over.

And where was Denzil? Surely, he hadn't legged it back to school and left him to face Madam Dish and the Hornblower alone?

He glanced anxiously at the door and wondered whether to make a break for it himself. But he'd left it too late. He squeezed his eyes shut and gave a little whimper as he felt a hand close over his shoulder.

Chapter Eight

WHEN HE DARED to open his eyes and twist his head round to see who the hand belonged to, Max had yet another shock. Denzil grinned back at him.

"You!" hissed Max. "You scared me half to death. Where have you been? And what about the diversion?"

"Sugar Dish's mum," grinned Denzil. "She's taking care of it now. It'll be ages before she's finished laying into the Hornblower."

"Keep your voice down," whispered Max, "and stop rustling the paper."

"Have you checked the advert?" said Denzil.

"I haven't even found it," said Max. "I didn't get the chance."

"Shift over," said Denzil. "Let me have a look."

Max shifted. There was no point in arguing. The thought of Mum – and the sight of Mr Hornby and

Mrs Cavendish together – had made his arms and legs turn to jelly. He leaned against the shelf and tried to stop himself shaking.

"Think I've got it," whispered Denzil, after a couple of minutes. "Computers and football, right?"

"That's it!" said Max.

"But what's a jingle mum?" said Denzil.

"Single mum," said Max.

"No. A jingle mum . . . with burly hair."

"No idea," said Max.

"Must be a mistake then," said Denzil.

Max snatched the paper and read the advert for himself.

'Jingle mum with burly hair, glasses and two wonderful children, seeks friendly slack man who likes computers, football and mousework.'

He stared at it. This wasn't a mistake. It was a disaster! A complete and absolute disaster.

"Look at it!" he cried, in dismay.

"Shut up!" hissed Denzil, but Max already knew he'd blown it.

A moment later, he watched in horror as two heads appeared over the top of the shelves and the disaster turned into a national state of emergency.

"Max Thompson!" cried Shirley-Anne. "What on earth are you doing here?"

"Oy! You!" roared Mr Hornby. "I told you once. Clear off. And get your hands off my news-papers."

"Oh, sh . . . sugar!" yelled Denzil. "Let's get out of here!"

Max knew it was the best idea Denzil had had in ages but he was too shocked to move. Before he knew it, Denzil had disappeared through the door without him.

"On your feet!" ordered Shirley-Anne, as she tried to pull him up from the floor. "You're coming with me."

Still in a daze, Max allowed himself to be dragged out of the shop.

Mr Hornby stood in the doorway and yelled after them until they turned the corner into Mortimer Street. Shirley-Anne ignored him. She was far too busy yelling at Max.

She clipped along the pavement on her high heels, pulling him along behind her and shrieking at the top of her voice.

"Wait till your mother hears about this! Sneaking

out of school! Creeping round shops! Stealing news-papers!"

She ran out of steam at about the same time that Max finally came to his senses but, by then, they were inside the school gates.

Shirley-Anne lowered her voice, but her tone was icy and threatening.

"For heaven's sake, Max. Haven't you got anything to say for yourself?"

Max shook his head miserably.

"Right then," she snapped. "I'll let your mother tell me all about it later."

"No," croaked Max weakly, finding his voice at last. "Please don't tell her."

Shirley-Anne glared at him.

"Can you give me one good reason why I shouldn't?"

"It's a secret . . . a surprise for Mum," said Max – and immediately felt like kicking himself up the backside.

What had he said that for? Madam Dish couldn't keep a secret. He might as well have told the *Parkway Gazette* – and then begged them to make it front-page news!

Chapter Nine

NOTHING COULD HAVE prepared Max for what happened next. Shirley-Anne swept him up into her arms and squashed him against her chest.

"Oooh, Max," she purred. "How lovely. You're such a little sweetie."

Her spiky brooch dug into his cheek and the smell of her perfume caught in his throat. He choked and coughed and tried to wriggle free.

Shirley-Anne sniffed loudly. She might have been crying, but Max guessed she'd caught a whiff of *his* perfume – picked up from the gap behind the toilets.

She let go a little and held him at arm's length.

"A surprise?" she said. "Good heavens! Why didn't you say so? I won't breathe a word, Max. It'll be our little secret."

Max stared at her, gob-smacked, and she winked

at him! Then she gave him a last, little squeeze and began leading him towards the classroom.

Miss Finch was taking the register.

Shirley-Anne waved hello to Sugar and whispered something in Miss Finch's ear.

Denzil stifled a laugh and some of the others giggled and sniggered, behind their hands. Max hoped they hadn't been watching through the windows.

Miss Finch fluttered and turned pink and told him not to worry. It was like telling a dead man not to lie down!

"What happened?" whispered Denzil, as Max slid into his seat.

"I'll tell you later," said Max, playing for time.

He had to think about this one. He couldn't tell Denzil that Shirley-Anne had hugged him in the playground! And he'd never believe that she'd promised to keep her mouth shut.

He could hardly believe it himself. Maybe he'd been wrong about her all along.

After all, thought Max, he'd been wrong about Angus McDonald. He'd had a long chat with him about whether to advertise for a white man or a black man and he'd been full of good advice and ideas.

But the stupid man couldn't even correct a few simple typing mistakes – and now he was stuck with an advert for a *slack* man!

Max tried to focus his eyes on the blackboard and listen to what Miss Finch was saying about quadratic equations. He gave up after about twenty seconds and went back to worrying.

Usually, he told himself, he was right about people. He'd known from the age of two that his sister, Claire, was a bossy-boots and she'd never let him down yet. Except for the mistake he'd made with Angus McDonald – and hopefully with Shirley-Anne – he was a good judge of character.

At home-time, though, Max realised he'd made a mistake about someone else too.

As soon as Miss Finch was out of earshot, about half the class gathered round his desk and suddenly burst into a chorus of the 'Bear Hunt' song – except they'd changed the words.

"We're going on a man hunt, we're going on a man hunt. Gonna be a good one, gonna be a good one. It'll be fun, it'll be fun."

The others were singing 'Jingle Mum' to the tune of *Jingle Bells*!

Max stumbled to his feet and gazed out over the sea of chanting, taunting faces. Denzil was standing at the back, with one hand clutching a desk to hold himself up and the other clutching his stomach. He was roaring with laughter.

"Shut up!" yelled Max, as he pushed through the crowd.

"How could you tell them?" he spat at Denzil. "It's not funny, y'know."

"Oh, come on," howled Denzil, almost choking on the words. "It's brilliant. Can't you take a joke?"

Max felt himself beginning to tremble with rage. His heart was thumping. His eyes were stinging – and he knew what that meant. He had to get out. He wasn't giving anyone the satisfaction of seeing him blubber – especially Denzil Moses.

"You know what you can do, don't you?" he screamed. "You can get lost!"

He shoved Denzil out of the way, banged open the classroom door and pounded down the corridor towards the playground – and home.

Chapter Ten

THE NEXT MORNING when Max woke up, the knot of anger in his chest was still there, reminding him of how much he hated Denzil. He told Mum he had belly-ache.

"It'll be that new virus," said Mum, as she prised open his jaw and shoved a thermometer into his mouth. "Chronic hypochondria!"

Max tried to nod, but Mum grabbed him by the throat and prodded his neck to see if his glands were up.

"Alfonse will have kittens if I take the day off," she said. "We've got a blue rinse, two manicures and a demi-wave before lunch, and Brenda's on holiday in Clacton."

She ripped the thermometer out of his mouth and peered at it over her glasses.

"Ninety-eight degrees," she muttered. "I've never

understood all that centigrade and Fahrenheit stuff. You're either completely normal or about to hit boiling point!"

She pinned him down on the bed and felt his forehead.

"You are a bit hot," she said. "I suppose I could ask Shirl to look after you."

"No," said Max quickly. "Let me come to work with you. I can sit under one of the driers and read the magazines or something."

"I'm sure she won't mind," said Mum.

"Please, Mum," begged Max. "I'd rather come with you."

"I must be going soft," said Mum, shaking her curls. "Come on then, if you're sure."

Max *was* sure. He didn't want to go to school and face Denzil, but he definitely didn't want to spend another day with Madam Cavendish.

He tried to tell himself that sweeping the salon floor and passing hair clips and curlers to Alfonse might be fun, if he put his mind to it. It didn't do any good. All day, his mind was on Denzil and the man hunt, and he was bored brainless before Mum got on to the second manicure.

The weekend was even worse. On Saturday, Max practised penalty kicks by aiming at the sign on the wall of the flats that said 'No ball games allowed'. On Sunday, he stayed in his room and practised quadratic equations.

Mum was so worried that she practically forced him to watch 'The Sunday Match'. But his heart wasn't in it.

He knew life couldn't go on like this, of course, and it didn't.

On Sunday evening, the telephone rang. Max crept to the top of the stairs and strained his ears.

"He's not the only one," Mum was saying. "Yes, yes . . . he's been really miserable."

He wondered who she was blabbing his life-story to.

"Terrific," said Mum. "No, really . . . I'd love to come."

Shirley-Anne, decided Max. He hoped she remembered her promise.

"OK, Theo," said Mum. "We'll see you next Saturday then. 'Bye. Take care."

Theo? Theo? Max racked his brains and tried to remember where he'd heard the name.

"Max!" called Mum suddenly. "Why are you crawling around on the stairs?"

"Thought I'd spotted that contact lens you lost a few weeks ago," lied Max smoothly.

"That was Mr Moses," said Mum. "Inviting you to the game at Highbury next week."

"Denzil's dad?" said Max. "I can't go."

"Don't be daft, Max. I've already said yes. I'm coming too. Mr Moses is such a *lovely* man and I haven't seen him for ages."

"You can't go either," said Max, panicking. "He's married!"

"What's the matter with you?" said Mum. "Of course, he's married. Mrs Moses isn't coming though. She's taking the twins to the zoo."

"But you don't even like football," cried Max. "Last time you spent the whole ninety minutes moaning about the cold and the noise and the bad language."

"Max," said Mum patiently. "I'm not going to watch the football. I just want to spend some time with you – and Theo."

This is terrible, thought Max. Mum had no idea. There was no point spending time with Mr Moses.

He was already married. He had a wife and three children!

OK, he did want a new dad – but not like this. They couldn't just pinch Denzil's! Even if he was a complete and absolute dweeb.

Chapter Eleven

THE NEXT DAY, Max went back to school. He had a new plan and he was determined to get the man hunt back on course.

He stepped over the pile of jackets pretending to be a goal post, and a deadly kick from Becky Jenkins slammed the ball against his shins so hard it made his eyes water.

The match was supposed to be a friendly lunch-time kick-around but everyone leapt up and down and yelled as if it was a World Cup final.

"To me, Max! To me!"

"Which side are you on?"

"Over here, you idiot! Boot it away!"

Max watched the ball trickle towards the goal mouth. But he wasn't here to play soccer. He ignored the shouts and marched across the penalty area until he was face-to-face with Denzil.

"I want to talk to you!" he said.

"I knew you'd talk to me sooner or later," said Denzil, as he took off up the wing.

Max chased after him.

"I'm only talking to you because we've got a problem," he yelled.

"You're the one with a problem," yelled back Denzil, as he dodged between two mid-fielders. "No sense of humour!"

Paul Kelly passed the ball and Denzil booted it towards the goal. It missed by a mile, but it bounced off a defender and rolled over the back line.

Denzil steadied himself to take the corner.

"We've *both* got a problem," cried Max, as Denzil took a run at the ball. "My mum fancies your dad!"

Denzil mis-kicked. The ball rolled straight to Sugar Cavendish, playing for the other team, and she tore off with it in the opposite direction.

Denzil took his eyes off the game and looked at Max for the first time.

"How can she fancy my dad? He's married!"

"I told her that," said Max. "It didn't make any difference. She's coming to the match on Saturday just so she can see him."

"But she doesn't even like football. Last time she just moaned about . . ."

"I told her that too," cut in Max. "She's still coming."

"What're we going to do?" said Denzil.

Before Max could answer, there was a loud cheer. Sugar had scored a goal!

"We'll sort it out later," cried Denzil. "Four-nil! We're getting slaughtered. Come on, Max – we need you. Let's finish the game."

The way Max saw it, he didn't have much choice. Four goals down is serious! He ran off and got himself into position for the centre kick.

He played well. He scooped up an impossible cross from Denzil and scored a blinding goal. And just before the final whistle, he set up Jamal Beckford's equaliser from an indirect free kick.

His team-mates went crazy, leaping on him and Jamal from all directions.

Denzil had a big silly grin on his face and as they filed back into class, he threw a playful punch at Max's shoulder.

Max grinned back and began to tell him about the new plan.

"We've been trying to get the men to Mum," he said. "That was our first mistake."

He was about to list all their other mistakes when Miss Finch held up her hand for silence so she could take the register. Better get straight to the point.

"Thirty-five thousand people," he whispered. "Mainly men and mainly Arsenal supporters – and all in one place at the same time."

He paused. Denzil was eyeing him strangely, as if he'd suddenly turned into a Flat Feet United supporter.

"Highbury Stadium," explained Max. "We'll take Mum to the men – the right men. It's the perfect place for a man hunt."

"I thought the idea was to *stop* your mum coming to Highbury," said Denzil, "and what about the Lonely Hearts men?"

"Useless," whispered Max. "Forget them. The postwoman's been *three* times since the advert came out and all she's brought is junk mail and bills for Mum – and a postcard for Claire. I haven't had a single reply."

"Well, what about my dad?" said Denzil. "We can't stop *him* coming to Highbury."

"Give me a break," said Max. "I'm still working on that bit. Anyway, there are two of us again now and we've got four more days. We're bound to come up with something."

Chapter Twelve

TWO DAYS LATER, Max trudged home in the rain.

At school, Miss Finch was always wittering on about how two heads are better than one, and Mr Goddard was always ranting about team-work. But none of their ideas seemed to be working for him and Denzil. They still had no idea how to stop Mum chasing Mr Moses.

Claire let him into the flat and behind her, through the living room door, he caught sight of Mum – and all the Dishes!

That's just what I need, thought Max. A mass invasion of girls and women!

"What's the matter with you?" said Claire, when she saw his face.

Max wondered if she was trying to be friendly. He was dripping wet and miserable. Maybe she felt sorry for him.

"Everything," he said, jerking his thumb towards the living room.

"They won't bite," sneered Claire. "Don't be such a wimp!"

Max stared at her. She wouldn't know 'friendly' if it hit her in the eye!

He pushed past her and went inside.

"Hi, Max," said Mum. "Had a good day?"

"Not really," said Max.

"Oh dear. Maybe this'll cheer you up."

She slid her hand down the side of the sofa and pulled out a large brown envelope.

Max knew what it was even before he saw the *Parkway Gazette* emblem (a gormless-looking owl with glasses).

He snatched it out of Mum's hand before she had a chance to recognise it. But Shirley-Anne's eyes were sharper than Mum's. She winked at him furiously and tapped the side of her nose a couple of times.

Max wondered how many bad spy movies she'd seen. Then he wondered how Mum could sit right next to her and not notice all the ridiculous faces she was pulling.

Then Mum noticed.

"What's going on? Did I miss something?"

"No," said Max quickly.

"He's up to something," said Charlotte.

"You should see him at school," said Sugar.

"For heaven's sake!" said Shirley-Anne. "Leave the boy alone. He's allowed the odd secret, isn't he?"

Max glared at her. This had gone far enough. He clutched the envelope tighter and fled upstairs to his room to open it.

Inside, there was a small blue envelope with a number on the front, a five pound note, and a slip of paper with another picture of the gormless owl.

Underneath the owl was a scribbled note:

Dear Max,
Only one reply I'm afraid. Partly my fault, but you did mention that you'd come top in a recent spelling test! Please accept my apologies – and a refund.
Good luck and best wishes,
Angus McDonald.
P.S. The letter's for your burly mum, not you!

Max put the fiver into his cash box and threw the note into the bin. ·

He stared at the blue envelope.

Angus was right, he supposed. If anyone was going to open it, it had to be Mum.

But not yet!

He stuffed it in the cash box with the money and went back downstairs.

He could hear Claire laughing with the others in the living room. She was probably telling them all what a wimp he was.

In the kitchen Max took out the bread knife – and stabbed the loaf. Then he hacked off a couple of slices to make a banana sandwich.

Just wait! He'd show them! Come Saturday, he'd be at Highbury Stadium, picking out a man. Maybe even one of the players. They were a bit young for Mum, but that was her problem. He wanted someone who could still kick a ball about in the park.

He'd choose someone tall and handsome – that'd suit Mum. Someone with a snazzy car and loads of money – that'd suit everyone. And to suit himself, thought Max, he'd be black – and he definitely wouldn't be a wimp!

Just a few more weeks and Mum'd be getting married and the man could move in. No more slushy films when there was soccer or an action movie on the other side. No more Sunday breakfasts or cosy evenings with the Dishes. If he was really lucky, no more Dishes!

Max took a bite of his sandwich and his vision of ideal family life suddenly shattered. Yuck! The banana tasted all right, but he'd gone over the top with the salad cream!

Chapter Thirteen

It WAS STILL raining on Saturday morning.

Claire was getting ready to go ice-skating.

"You must be mad!" she said. "Standing about watching football in this weather."

"We'll be sitting down," said Max.

"It's OK," said Mum. "I'm well prepared."

By mid-day, the rain had eased, but Max wanted to die when he saw Mum's preparations.

She was wearing a pair of old riding boots, a bright yellow plastic mac and a matching hat!

They met Denzil and his dad at the tube station and somehow Mr Moses didn't notice that Mum looked like a cross between Farmer Giles and Captain Hook. He gave her a huge hug, as they set off towards the stadium.

Max and Denzil dived in between them, before

they did anything even more stupid – like kissing or holding hands!

"Arsenal's the only tube station in London named after a football club," said Mr Moses, over the top of their heads.

"Is it really?" said Mum.

"It used to be Gillespie Road but . . ."

"Ignore them," whispered Denzil. "I've finally got it sussed. He'll talk football facts all afternoon. She'll be bored silly. There's no way she'll still fancy him."

Max glanced up at Mum. She didn't look bored. She was beaming like a lighthouse!

They reached the ground and found their seats, but Mr Moses didn't let up. He pointed out all the new features in the stadium. Then Mum asked him where the ladies' toilets were. That stopped him dead. He didn't have a clue.

Mum went to find them and by the time she got back, the game had already started. Mr Moses began to explain it but Mum ignored him and roared at the top of her voice.

"Come on, you Reds!"

Denzil was right, thought Max. Mum was fed up

with Mr Moses already. She wanted to watch the match in peace, like the rest of them.

But Mum was anything but peaceful.

"You plonker!" she bellowed, when one of the Arsenal strikers missed an early chance.

Mum yelled at the referee and the linesmen as well as all the players, and when Arsenal finally found the net, she went berserk!

'Did you see the number eight?" she cried. "What a goal!"

Mr Moses looked startled but Max felt himself relax. Things were going really well. The score was one-nil. The number eight shirt belonged to the brilliant black striker – and with all Mum's noise and that outfit, it could only be a matter of time before he noticed her.

At half-time, Mum was completely red in the face, but she leapt out of her seat and charged off to fetch drinks – without Mr Moses.

"I'm going to find her," said Max, after about ten minutes. "She might be stuck in another queue for the loo."

She wasn't. She was at the back of the stand,

leaning across the counter of the kiosk, laughing and chatting with the tea-lady.

"Max," called Mum, as she glanced round and spotted him. "Come and meet Kimani."

Max went closer. It wasn't a tea-lady at all. It was a tea-man!

"This is my son, Max," said Mum. "The one I was telling you about."

"Hi, Max," said Kimani. "Good match, eh?"

Max looked up at him. His face was smooth and dark and it broke into a warm, friendly smile which made his eyes sparkle.

Max only realised he was staring when Mum poked him in the ribs with her elbow.

"Say hello, then," she prompted. "And take these things back. I'll be there in a minute."

She pushed two cans of cola into his pockets, two cups of tea into his hands and four packets of crisps under his chin.

Max said "Hello," which wasn't easy with his bottom jaw out of action. And as he staggered back to the seats, he made a quick decision.

The players were down on the pitch, miles away. But here was a perfectly acceptable black man, right within striking distance. He even worked for the Arsenal!

Mum was gone for ages and she missed the only other goal of the match – a superb header from one of the mid-fielders, to make it two-nil.

"Kimani seemed nice," said Max, when she finally came back. "You should've asked him to go out or something."

"I did!" smiled Mum. "He's bringing take-away pizza round for dinner on Wednesday."

Chapter Fourteen

KIMANI HAD SWAPPED his Arsenal jacket for an African print shirt. And he seemed to know all about their taste in pizzas.

The big one for him and Mum had olives and anchovies popping out all over it, like a rash. But he'd ordered two Hawaiian Surprises as well. Extra mushrooms for Claire and no surprise for Max – he hated pineapple.

Max licked the last crumbs of garlic bread off his fingers and began to stack the plates.

"We'll do that," said Mum, taking them out of his arms. "Come on, Claire. Give me a hand with the coffee and ice-cream. Then we can relax and let these two do the washing up."

While the others were busy in the kitchen, Kimani told Max how he'd met Mum years ago when she was in hospital having Claire.

He'd been working as a nurse but soon afterwards, he'd gone home to Tanzania.

"I came back a few months ago," said Kimani. "I'm working for an agency as a midwife now but some people are a bit funny about it – because I'm a bloke."

Max wasn't absolutely sure what midwives did – but he was pretty certain they didn't make hot dogs and cups of tea!

"What about the snack bar?" he asked.

"Oh, I just work at the Arsenal ground to earn extra money," said Kimani. "They've got a crèche too and sometimes I look after the babies instead. Depends where they need me."

Max couldn't believe his ears. *Babies.* Babies and hot dogs!

"Don't you like football?"

"Come on, man," laughed Kimani. "Of course I do. That's why I prefer the snack bar. I get to see the match as well. But I like kids too," he added, looking serious, "and the crèche is a good idea. You can't always count on the dads. Some of them would never stay at home with the babies."

There was a silence. Max knew all about not

being able to count on dads, but he didn't really want to talk about it.

Luckily, Mum and Claire came back with the pudding and drinks, so he didn't have to.

They talked about sport instead. Claire bragged about winning a bronze ice-skating medal and Kimani congratulated her as if she'd won gold at the Winter Olympics!

"Oh man," said Kimani, later, when they'd washed up. "I have to be at the hospital really early tomorrow. I'd better be going."

Max said goodbye and hurried upstairs. He crouched down behind the banister. It was the best place to listen out for the sound of snogging at the front door.

But all he heard was Mum saying, "Thanks for the pizzas. I'll see you on Saturday."

"What's happening on Saturday?" called Max, when Kimani had gone.

"I'm off to that new French restaurant in the High Street," said Mum. "Now go to bed."

*

"What d'you mean it's all over?" said Denzil, the next day. "I've told everyone your new step-dad plays for Arsenal. I've promised them tickets and everything!"

"Sorry," said Max. "I've decided on Kimani. He's perfect."

"Nobody's perfect," said Denzil. "We should at least check him against the list."

Denzil rummaged around in one of the drawers underneath the twins' bunk beds.

"Right!" he said, at last. "Full name?"

"Kimani Sanga," said Max.

"Age?"

"Not sure," said Max. "Younger than Mum."

"Thirty-ish," said Denzil. "Wheels?"

"Outland Warrior," said Max.

"Never heard of it," said Denzil. "Must be one of those new four-wheel-drive jeeps."

"Two-wheel," said Max. "It's a bike!"

Denzil rolled his eyes and wrote it down.

"Job?"

"Midwife," said Max.

"Midwife!" shrieked Denzil. "You mean he pulls out babies?"

"He makes tea and baby-sits too," said Max. "But don't you dare say he's a wimp! He used to play for the Tanzanian national youth team and he still plays Sunday league."

"That's a tick for football," said Denzil. "What about computers?"

"No idea," said Max, "but like you said, nobody's perfect!"

Chapter Fifteen

On saturday, mum broke her all-time record for the number of hours spent in the bathroom.

She took so long that every now and then, Max tiptoed upstairs and listened for the sound of splashing to make sure she hadn't drowned.

Afterwards, he kept a look-out for Kimani through the living-room window, while Mum got dressed in the bedroom.

Max groaned when he saw her. Talk about going over the top! She was wearing a shiny purple dress and dangly earrings. Her eyelids were purple too, and she'd swapped her glasses for her new contact lenses.

"Mum!" he said. "You look really . . . really different."

"Different?" said Claire, looking up from the television. "She looks brilliant!"

Max pulled a face and took out the bottle he'd been hiding in his pocket.

"Here," he said. "I got you a surprise."

"Midnight Serenade," said Mum, reading the label. "Genuine French perfume."

Max watched anxiously as she opened the bottle and sniffed.

"That *is* a surprise," said Mum. "Thanks, Max. Now I'll *smell* different too."

Max smiled to himself. He'd been to the Hornblower's shop and spent nearly two pounds from the money he'd got back from Angus McDonald. But hopefully the perfume would finally put a stop to Shirley-Anne pretending to be a double-agent and dropping hints to Mum about secrets and surprises.

He gazed through the window again, into the darkness. He felt his chest fill with pride and success.

He'd done it! The man hunt was over! Any minute now, Kimani would arrive, looking handsome in a smart suit and shiny shoes – or a long African shirt and matching trousers.

The doorbell rang. "I'll get it!" cried Max, already skidding up the hallway.

He threw open the door – and stared.

Something was wrong. Kimani was wearing faded jeans and muddy trainers and his Arsenal jacket!

Mum'll go berserk, thought Max. Where are his posh restaurant clothes?

"Hey, Max. What's happening?"

"Good question," muttered Max, as Kimani came in and headed for the living room.

He almost crashed into Mum, but he stepped back just in time and flashed her a smile.

"You look different," he said.

"Hi," said Mum, looking pleased and speaking in a normal voice. "Thanks."

Max stared even harder. Then he hung on to the door handle for support as Shirley-Anne suddenly swept into the flat.

It was one of those moments when the world seemed to be spinning out of control at supersonic speed, but his brain had gone into slow motion. What was going on?

"Pooh! What's that stink?" screeched Shirley-Anne. "Smells like a rat died!"

"Let's go," said Mum, grabbing her coat from the

hook. "Our table's booked for eight. Brenda's waiting. We'll be late."

Max watched in a daze, as Kimani kissed Mum on the cheek, Shirley-Anne wobbled on her high heels, and everybody said goodbye. WHAT WAS GOING ON?

And then the answer hit him like a clap round the head with a baseball bat!

Mum was going out with Madam Dish! Kimani was here to baby-sit! The man hunt wasn't over!

"Wait!" yelled Max.

He didn't mean to say it. It just popped out while his brain was still in neutral.

"Wait, I've got something else for you."

He dashed upstairs, grabbed the blue envelope out of his cash box and charged down again.

"What's this?" said Mum. "Another surprise?"

Max handed the letter to Mum and watched while she tore it open and read it. Then she laughed and pushed it back at him.

"Very funny, Max. But we're in a rush. Next, you'll be trying to fix me up with Mr Moses or Kimani. What a joke!"

"It's *not* a joke," said Max, as he looked down

from Mum's smiling, red face to the crumpled, blue letter in his hands.

But when he looked up again, the hallway was empty. Everyone was gone.

Chapter Sixteen

Max slammed the front door and slumped into a heap at the bottom of the stairs.

He glanced at the letter again. All that hard work, he thought, as he screwed it up into a tight little ball and hurled it against the wall. All for nothing!

He'd never understand women, he decided. How could Mum think it was a joke?

He was just beginning to think it would serve her right if she got French food poisoning from the frogs' legs and snails when the doorbell rang again.

She was back! She'd come to say sorry. She was going to contact the Lonely Hearts man right away. And maybe, thought Max, just maybe, he'd forgive her.

"Oh," he said gloomily, when he saw who it was. "Come in. Join the party."

"Oh, no!" cried Denzil. "Are you having one too?"

It took a good five minutes before Max had any idea what Denzil was talking about.

It turned out that Denzil's entire family (one grandmother, two grandfathers, three aunties, six uncles and so many cousins he'd lost count) had come round to celebrate his mum and dad's wedding anniversary.

"Dad says there's no way we're watching 'Match of the Day' in the middle of a party," said Denzil. "If your mum's out with Kimani, I thought we could gang up on Claire and watch it here."

"Mum's gone out with Shirley-Anne," said Max. "Kimani's here."

"That's three against one," said Denzil. "Brilliant!"

Max lost his temper.

"Don't you get it?" he exploded. "Mum's gone out with Shirley-Anne!"

He scooped up the letter with the toe of his trainer and kicked it towards Denzil.

"And she thought the Lonely Hearts letter was a joke!" he added angrily.

"Well, I did try to warn you," said Denzil, as he bent down and picked it up.

"What d'you mean?" said Max.

"She doesn't fancy Kimani or my dad," said Denzil. "They're her friends. She doesn't want to marry them. She doesn't want to marry anyone. That's why she wears that T-shirt."

"T-shirt?" said Max, amazed.

"Y'know. The one that says a woman needs a man like a fish needs a bicycle."

"I don't care if she needs a man or not!" cried Max. "What about me? I need one!"

"Maybe you've already got one," said Denzil. "Didn't you say Kimani was here?"

Max watched as Denzil calmly smoothed out the letter against his leg and began to read.

And in the silence that followed, Max realised that Denzil was right. Kimani *was* here. In the living room. Sitting on the sofa. Watching television.

It didn't matter if Mum didn't want a man. If he was honest, the man hunt wasn't about what Mum wanted. It was about himself.

And now, realised Max, it really was over. He'd got exactly what he wanted.

"No wonder your mum thought this was a joke," cried Denzil suddenly.

His face was split by a huge grin and his shoulders were beginning to shake.

"It's signed by someone we know!"

"Who?" demanded Max.

"Mr Goddard!" cried Denzil, exploding with laughter. "Says he likes chasing mice and he loves burly women!"

Max gasped. He had a horrible vision of Mr Goddard wobbling round the flat, bellowing orders and filling the air with his terrible breath. Talk about a lucky escape!

"Max!" called out Kimani, from the living room. "Come on, man. What're you doing out there? 'Match of the Day' is just starting."

"You were right," laughed Denzil, as he headed for the living room. "He's perfect!"

Not perfect, thought Max, as he followed him. None of them were perfect.

Kimani didn't have a clue about computers. Mum had a whole heap to learn about boys growing up into men. Denzil couldn't deliver a decent cross from the left wing. Claire was still a bossy-boots. The

Dishes still hadn't moved to Mars. And Arsenal were a long way from the top of the table.

No, life definitely wasn't perfect, decided Max. But, oh, man, it was heading in the right direction.